Dream On

by

Bali Rai

First published in 2002 in Great Britain by
Barrington Stoke Ltd,
18 Walker Street, Edinburgh EH3 7LP

www.barringtonstoke.co.uk

This edition published 2007

ISBN: 978-1-84299-550-1

Printed in Great Britain by Bell & Bain Ltd

A Note from the Author – Bali Rai

The idea for *Dream On* came from a TV programme about the fact that there are no Asian players in the Football League. I wanted to show in this story that young British Asians also want to follow in the footsteps of Michael Owen and David Beckham.

Coaches and scouts often have wrong ideas about Asian players and so they don't promote them. They think they lack physical strength, motivation and ambition. And after all, they'll go off and become dentists, lawyers and doctors in the end, won't they? I know that was how it was when I was at school, and that was 15 years ago!

This story also makes up for my own unfulfilled ambition to play for Liverpool FC. Not that I was ever good enough – but we can dream! I hope you enjoy it.

To Penny and Jennifer Luithlen, all at Barrington Stoke and to all the pupils who participated in the editorial process.

To Liverpool FC for 25 years of pleasure.

To my mum and my sister for their continued support and finally to Jeff Allen and Baby-Jane Sykes.

Thank you all.

Contents

Chapter 1
Fish and Chips

"Do I have to work in the shop today, daddy-ji?" I asked my dad.

Man, I hated working in my old man's fish and chip shop. It was boring and smelly. And oily too. Loads of kids from my school came in and all I ever got from them was, "Chips an' curry sauce, mate!"

When I was younger, it was quite funny, being asked for that all the time. But after a while, it just got on my nerves. It wasn't strictly a fish and chip shop either. My old man sold Indian style food too – samosas and pakora and kebabs, and curries of course. For years, I thought he had the only chippy in England that was really an Indian takeaway in disguise. Until one of my uncles opened one in Birmingham.

"This is how we making our money, beteh," my old man would say to me in his own peculiar brand of English. "Those trainers you are wearing were paid for by fish an' chips."

"Yeah, I know that, Dad, but I wanna go out with me mates."

"Out? Out where? I paying you money to work, do your duty to the family, make sure that you finish your homework, and all you asking is go out. Tell me, beteh, do your friends pay you to go out? Eh?"

"Don't be silly, Dad. And anyway, I need a life outside of this place. Otherwise how am I supposed to grow up like a normal person? Man, I'll probably turn into a battered fish before I escape from here."

My dad looked at me like I was proper mad. Crazy.

"Now who is being stupid boy? If you want outside life? How about school?"

"Ah man, you ain't even listening, Dad. What's the point of talking to you?"

"I am listening, Baljit. Now pass me that bucket of chips and go and get some frozen samosas from your mother." Dismissed. Just like that.

I went over to the big, yellow bucket into which I had thrown what felt like a million chipped potatoes earlier, and dragged it over to my dad. I wasn't going to pick it up. Man, raw chips weigh a ton. Over the counter, I saw our first customer come in. It was Mr Biggs, a pensioner who lived up the street.

I knew it would be Mr Biggs. He was always our first customer. He always wore his old, brown, leather shoes, and the same pair of faded, brown, pinstripe trousers with brown braces, and a cream coloured shirt, tucked in. This was finished off with a grey overcoat and a grey felt hat which Mr Biggs told me was called a fedora.

I felt sorry for him. I remember when his wife died, when I was younger, and for about two months he didn't come into the shop. My old man was worried about him and asked all our neighbours if they had seen him. No-one had. And then one day he was back, only he looked older and more frail, and he smelt kind of musty.

Since then, my dad only charges him for his chips on Monday, though he comes in every day. Monday's when he gets his pension. Dad thinks giving Mr Biggs free meals is a way of doing his duty as a Sikh.

Part of the Sikh religion is to provide a free kitchen to those less fortunate than you, no matter what colour or religion they are. It's called the *langar*. My old man provides it for Mr Biggs and another pensioner, Mrs Benjamin, who's Jamaican. But no-one else.

"Be out of the business if I did," he always tells me.

Mr Biggs waited, like he did every day, for the first batch of chips to come out of the fryer, and spoke to my dad about the war, and the way that the whole area that we lived in seemed to have changed for the worse.

There was rubbish on the streets, he said, and cracks in the pavement and the council just didn't care. What if he fell over some rubbish lying around, or caught his toe on a crack and broke his neck falling over? Who'd look after his poor wife, Elsie, then? Heh?

Then my old man reminded him that Elsie was dead. Mr Biggs nodded and looked kind of sad. They spoke some more and then Mr Biggs ordered chips. "None of that curry sauce mind. That's for you rag heads. I'll have a little tub of gravy, Mr Sandhu."

My old man laughed at the way Mr Biggs called us rag heads. I didn't think it was funny, joking about turbans. But my old man told me that old dogs can't be taught new tricks, only he had a Punjabi version, which involved a long story about a lazy, old water buffalo and a young herder with a big stick. He told me that Mr Biggs wasn't really a racist – he just didn't know there were some things you just didn't say.

"I would rather he calling me the rag head than he throwing petrol in my shop, beteh."

By which I think he meant that words can't hurt you.

He gave Mr Biggs his food and said, "No money, please," like he always did.

"Ay, you're a good 'un. I'll have to get you a good bottle of whisky one day, Mr Sandhu." This was Mr Biggs' usual reply.

Then he turned to me and smiled. "All right, kid? How's the footie going?"

"It would be good if the old man let me out of here for once," I replied, ducking as Dad threw an oily chip at me.

"Make a lot of money playin' football these days," Mr Biggs said. And then he turned and walked to the door still talking. God knows who he was talking to. "Ah, course, in my day ..." he was saying.

****

I worked in the shop almost every night. I'd get home from school, eat and then do two hours of homework or reading. I had to. My old man made me.

7

"Knowledge is power, Baljit." He believed that education would make me a better man. That and getting oily and sweaty and smelly in a chippy.

And I wished he'd call me Jit for short because I hated Baljit. But my old man would rather not speak to me at all than call me by the name all my friends used.

I enjoyed working in the chippy as a kid. It was like a great big adventure and my dad was the action hero. I remember seeing tanked up blokes coming in, calling my dad all kinds of racist names, and he would just smile and take their money.

If they got really nasty he'd tell them to 'leaving my shop you'. Or sometimes he'd go bright red, grab the big, old kebab knife from under the steel counter and go through the hatch, into the shop.

My dad is a big man and not one person stood their ground when he went mad.

They just left, scattering their chips on the floor, curry sauce an' all.

It was when I started to get into playing footie that I began to mind working in the shop. I got to stay behind after school for practice on Wednesday nights and was allowed to play for the school team on Saturday mornings, but nothing beyond that.

My two best mates, Dave and Mo, played with me for the school team. They also played Sunday League games for a local side which had really good links with the talent scouts from major clubs like Leicester City and Aston Villa. They went to more practice sessions than me and played more games. I wanted to do that too.

But my old man just told me I was silly. "You playing one night in week and Saturday morning. That is enough, beteh."

"But Dad, I wanna play more games, like Mo and Dave. I love playin'. It's not like I'm out stealing cars and taking drugs every night! I just wanna play football."

"And I just want pay the bills, innit?"

"But how am I ever going to get as good as Emile Heskey? You wouldn't complain if I ended up signing for Liverpool, would you?"

"I never see even one Indian playing the football. They don't letting us into the teams, innit."

"Only because people like you stop people like me havin' a go!" I was getting angry.

"*Chadd deh*, Baljit," he said, which means 'leave it'. And then he threw another chip at me, one which was covered in batter, that hit me in the middle of my forehead. The batter dripped down my face. Well, after that, how could I not burst into laughter and throw one back at him?

Chapter 2
A Chance?

It was Dave and Mo that told me about the trials at Leicester City. We all played together for the school team and our coach, Mr Ball, was also a youth team coach for Leicester. He looked after the under 14s team.

One of his jobs was to go around to different schools and look for talented players. He had mentioned an open trial for under 16s and told Mo that he thought all three of us would have a great chance of being picked for the team. When they told me, I got really excited.

Ever since I started playing football, I've always had this dream about becoming a professional footballer playing for Liverpool. I've loved them since I was a kid.

But as soon as I started dreaming about what might happen in the future, I remembered my old man. There was no way he'd let me be a professional footballer. He wanted me to become a lawyer or a doctor. "These are the good jobs, Baljit. Never mind the football. If you dream it must be for real. Why can't you dream about things that really matter?" That was his usual reply.

I was going to have to do something to convince him I was serious.

****

I suppose I'd better tell you a bit more about my two best mates. Dave is my oldest friend. We have been at school together since we were five years old. He looks like a 15-year-old Eddie Murphy – you know, the actor – and he's funny too. He can find a joke for any moment, although some of them are really bad. His birthday is only one day after mine and we are very similar.

Mo is Asian like me. His parents are from Pakistan and he moved to our school when he was 12. He used to live in Oldham, near Manchester. That's why he's a Man United fan. In fact, I'm quite surprised we get on so well, as Man U are the sworn enemies of Liverpool. He takes the mick out of me all the time because his team wins everything and we've done quite badly recently. But that's all changing now. I keep telling Mo that his boys have had their time. It's time for a change.

Dave just laughs at us both. "I don't care who wins what, man," he always tells us. "I just wanna play for them so I can earn the kind of money that Emile Heskey is on."

Mo is a bit more serious than either me or Dave, specially when it comes to football. He likes to push himself and we call him Mr Motivator because when we play together he's always urging us on, telling us to run faster, try harder. It's like having a teacher as your best mate. Strange. He's cool though.

We'd just finished school for the day when Dave and Mo told me about the trials. We were on our way home through some playing fields. They belonged to another school, our local rivals. The estate we lived on was on the other side of the fields. A narrow alley led from the last field into the shopping area where my dad's chippy was.

We were playing a dangerous game walking home that way. The kids from the other school would have jumped us if they had seen us. But we were too busy talking about the trials to be bothered.

"He ain't gonna let me go to them," I told Dave and Mo, talking about my old man.

Dave looked at me like I was mad. "Course he is, man. Like he's gonna stop you."

"Dave's right, you know," said Mo. "Man, if my dad thought I might make it into the Leicester team, he'd start dreaming about how much money he'd be able to send home to Pakistan, to buy more land that he don't even need."

Dave just grinned. "Boy, you ain't even got to the trial, Mo, and already you're dreaming about being the first Pakistani lad to play for Moneybags United."

"You know what I mean," answered Mo. "My old man is sure that we're gonna get kicked out of this country. That's why he sends all his money back to Pakistan."

"It'll be your money not his, if you ever do make it," I said.

"Yeah and I ain't goin' to leave this country. This is my home. Think I'm gonna play international games for Pakistan?"

"Hey, daydreamer, there you go again. No-one ain't asked you to play for England *Ladies* yet – never mind anyone else!" Dave was grinning again.

"Least I'd play the ladies," replied Mo. "You'd be too busy tryin' to get in their shorts."

"Ain't nothing wrong with that. A healthy thing for any young man to do," Dave replied. He wasn't serious.

Mo scowled. "Why does every serious conversation we have end up being about girls?"

"Because you is too serious an' the ladies be what life is all about, man," said Dave.

"Your life, maybe."

I listened as Mo and Dave had a go at each other, but I was more interested in the trials. I wanted more details.

"So when is the first session?" I asked, trying to change the subject.

"Next week. Mr Ball is gonna drive us to it. It's at the training ground," replied Mo.

"What? The Leicester City training ground?"

"Yeah."

"Wicked!" A trial at a Premiership club. Now I was excited. I was going and that was that. My old man was just going to have to lump it.

We heard shouting behind us. I turned and saw about eight lads from the other school running towards us. They looked like they were older than us.

Dave saw them too. "Hey you two, forget your serious chat and run!" he shouted and took off. I followed him.

Mo turned and saw the gang of lads. "Flipping heck," he said as he swung his bag onto his shoulder and set off behind us.

We ran for the alley that took us into the shopping area. It was about the distance of a football pitch away and we were running like hell. I felt something whizz past my ear. It was half a brick. Man, these lads weren't messing about.

As I ran, I was trying to work out what we had done to them to make them attack us. And then I heard one of them shouting racist abuse at us. They were gaining on us.

Dave got to the alley first, with me right behind him. I turned to see if Mo was OK, just as he slipped and fell forwards, grazing one side of his face on the gravel.

I stopped and ran back to him. He was shaking. I helped him up. The gang, who were all white lads, were about fifty yards away. I was wetting myself. "Mo, come on! COME ON!"

We set off again as more stones – smaller this time – flew past us. One of them caught me behind the ear and made it sting, but I ignored it. I don't know what we had done to our attackers, but I wasn't going to stop and ask them. I don't mind getting into a fight if the odds are fair. Eight lads against three though. Forget that, man!

As Mo and I ran towards the shops I saw that Dave had reached my old man's takeaway. He was coming out, my dad behind him, sleeves rolled up and my mum's chapati rolling pin in his hand.

We ran up to them and my dad told us to get into the shop. Mo went in, but Dave and I didn't want to miss the action. Dad headed for the alley to have a go at the gang of lads and I wasn't going to let him go alone. Nor was Dave. We went after him.

The white lads reached the end of the alley and stopped as soon as they saw my old man. One of our neighbours, Mr Smith, who runs the video store, came out and stood next to my dad. He was a retired policeman and he liked to think that the shopping area was his beat.

When the lads saw him too they swore a few times, called us some more racist names and told us to stay off their fields. Then they turned and ran, just as my dad swore in Punjabi and ran towards them, holding the rolling pin in front of him. Man, the sight of him would have scared the hell out of anyone. All of a sudden I was really proud of him.

He turned back when he got to the alley, having made sure that the gang had gone, and came back to where Dave and me were standing with Mr Smith.

"Them effing kids," Mr Smith remarked. "I'd like to give their parents a piece of my ..."

"Parents more stupid then the kids, innit," replied my dad. "If my boy done that, I beat him me own self."

"Man, that was scary," said Dave. He looked shaken but angry too. "See, when I catch them boys ..."

"They'll give you the beating they couldn't give you today," I said, finishing his sentence.

"Them boys not worth the hassle, innit," my dad said. He walked off towards the video shop with Mr Smith, both of them moaning about how bad this country was getting. I turned and went back to our shop, hoping that Mo wasn't too badly hurt.

He was standing by the counter with a tissue pressed to his face. It wasn't too bad.

He had a few scratches but nothing fatal. I took him into the back and cleaned his face up with a bit of cotton wool. Then he went home with Dave, who was still really angry.

Chapter 3
Mandip's Plan

The following Saturday I got home from a match against another school team, to find that the shop was closed. It was just gone one o'clock in the afternoon. Normally, my old man opened for about three hours over lunch on Saturday and Sunday to catch what he called 'week ending trade'. At first I thought that something was wrong, but when I walked into the house it was full of people.

My uncle Ranjit and his family had come to visit from Birmingham. Real Brummies, they were. His wife had just had a baby boy and they had decided to celebrate.

My uncle had two older kids, a lad called Jagdip and a girl called Mandip. Jagdip was 12 and he did my head in. He was at that awful age where he asked questions every five seconds about anything and everything. Mandip was my age and she was really quiet and shy. I knew she didn't like family visits because she had to wear proper Punjabi outfits and she was always telling me that she felt like a circus clown in them.

"People just stare at you, man." Every time she told me that it made me laugh. Partly because it was funny, but mostly because she had a thick Brummie accent.

My uncle was similar to my old man. Big and strong, and he liked to drink. He owned a car repair garage and was always going on about the last job he'd had or the latest Ford this or BMW that. But he was quite a good laugh. He was in the living room when I got in and he got up and gave me a big bear hug that squeezed the air out of me. "Baljit, beteh. How are you? Working hard for your father, eh?"

My dad laughed at that. He pointed to the coffee table which was loaded with Indian food. Samosas and pakora and a plate of tandoori chicken as well as tea and glasses of mango juice.

"Eat something with us, Baljit. Your uncle has a new baby boy," he said, proudly.

My uncle nodded and slapped my shoulder. "You getting close to the age where you gonna be giving us grandkids soon, innit," he said, knowing that it would wind me up.

I shook my head at him. "Not before I become a footballer, uncle-ji. Maybe after that."

My uncle laughed.

"The football. That all he care about," said my dad.

"And how that all going?" My uncle asked the question, but he really wasn't that interested. He picked up a samosa and stuffed half of it into his mouth before I got a chance to reply.

"All right. My coach says I could become a pro – if *he* let me." I nodded at the old man.

"You forget the football, beteh. You wanna get good trade like me or your dad. People always need good mechanic, and these whites always gonna buy the fish an' chips."

"I don't want to sell chips an' that, man. I wanna be a star."

"Well, when you make the first million pounds, you not forgetting your poor uncle-ji." And then my uncle laughed again and started to talk to my old man about boring stuff.

I told them that I was going to my room to get changed and I went off, wondering if it was a good time to bring up the footie trial, with my dad being in a good mood and that. In the end I decided against it. With my uncle there it would be like going up against two dads not one. Hardly the best odds for the game I wanted to play.

I stayed in my room for a bit, thinking. How was I going to convince my dad to let me go to the school practice on Wednesday night *and* the trials on Thursday evening?

My pest of a cousin came up to my room and tried to get in but I wasn't having it.

"What you doin' in there, bhai-ji," he asked me about ten times, as he stood outside my bedroom door. 'Bhai-ji' means brother and he had to call me that because I was older than him and his old man had told him he had to show respect for me.

"I ain't doin' anything, Jagdip. Go away," I yelled through the door.

"You got a computer in there? Can I play on it?" He wouldn't go away.

"Yes and no. I have got a computer, but you can't have a go on it. I ain't got no games anyway. I use it for my homework," I said, lying.

"You're lyin' – I seen you playin' on it last time we come 'ere. Let me play." He just wouldn't stop whining.

"Get lost, you little brat."

"I'm tellin' me dad."

"Oh get lost – I'm busy!"

I heard him walk off, and then his sister Mandip knocked in his place. I let her in because she was kind of cool and we got on well.

"Ain't you comin' down?" she asked, as she sat down at my desk.

"Nah, Mandip. Can't be bothered. They bore me, talking about money all the time."

"Tell me about it." Her Brummie accent was so thick that I wanted to laugh. I had to stop myself from copying it too. Man, she would have killed me if I had.

"Don't even wanna be 'ere. My friends was goin' up Birmingham centre and I wanted to go with 'em."

"But – now let me guess – you *had* to come here. Family coming before friends, innit."

I was talking just like our fathers did. We both laughed.

"Man, them two talk exactly the same, innit," Mandip said.

"I just wanna go to this football trial at Leicester City on Thursday. But my dad thinks footie is a waste of time."

"Leicester City? You mean the real thing?" she asked me, raising her eyebrows.

"Yeah."

"You *that* good?" She looked amazed.

"I dunno. That's what I was hoping to find out," I told her.

"Man. Imagine if you got to play it for proper. All that *money* you could get."

"Don't think I ain't thought about it," I said.

"But you *are* the only son an' your dad probably wants to pass the business on to you and all that." Mandip shook her head.

"Exactly. Or he wants me to be the lawyer and the doctor. Make him prouding." I was copying Dad's peculiar English and his accent.

She laughed because I did it so well. "You *got* to go then."

"How? I'm already playing on Wednesday night. He ain't gonna let me out Thursday. I'll be working in the shop."

"Just make up a story, man. That's what I do when I wanna go out."

It was my turn to be amazed. "What? I thought you was all shy and that?" My cousin Mandip, the secret raver. Cool.

"Yeah, good cover, innit? *They* think what you did – that I'm the quiet type. Into books. My local library don't close till *eleven* some nights," she said with a wink.

"I can't believe how sly you are," I said, impressed.

"Don't knock it, Jit. You ain't a girl. I got it harder than you." It's true. Punjabis are stricter on girls. Family honour and all that. Still, I had to hand it to my cousin. She'd come up with a winning idea.

"So what excuse do I use?" I asked her.

"Someone's birthday?" she suggested. "A party?"

"Nah, they know when my best mates' birthdays are."

"School trip, then. Say you're going to London. Won't be back till late."

I thought about it for a bit. It would need a bit of work but it was good.

"Yeah, that's the one. Cheers, Mandip – you're a star. I owe you one."

"Forget it, Jit. Just buy me some wicked gear when you sign up for Liverpool, man." She smiled and got up from the chair. "Come on, Michael Owen, we'd best get back to the fun and games. They'll be asking where we got to."

I smiled and followed my cousin downstairs. "Where did you get those trousers, off a clown?" I was poking fun at her traditional Punjabi suit. I got a sharp elbow in my ribs for my trouble.

Chapter 4
The Plan in Action

Later the same evening, I told Mo and Dave about the plan to con my old man into thinking that we were going on a school science trip instead of to the trials. They both laughed at me to begin with but then they saw that I was being serious and agreed to help. Dave told me that he'd print out a letter from the school for me on his new computer.

Mo came into the shop at about eight that night and pretended that he had been given the letter for me but had forgotten to hand it over. When my dad asked where we were going to visit, Mo, quick as usual, said the Science Museum and the British Library and my old man was really impressed.

"Good to learn things. Better than kicking the balls, innit."

He said the last bit so fast that it sounded like something else, and me and Mo cracked up with laughter. I was laughing too at the way he'd fallen for our scam so easily.

He must have been in a good mood because he told me that the shop was closing early and would I put a handwritten sign in the window to say so. My uncle and his family were still with us and my old man wanted to get plastered. When I asked him what to write he sighed and told me to 'thinking you self'. That made Mo laugh and then my dad threw a soggy chip at him, which hit his ear. At that I started laughing.

"Telling you boys what." My dad was smiling and looking at Mo. "Today I not working. I celebrating Ranjit's new baby boy, innit."

"And?" I could sense something coming.

"How your friend like tenner to help you in shop tonight?"

I looked at Mo, whose face lit up at the mention of money. "Up to you, man," I said, realising that we'd have a right good laugh in the shop.

"Yeah, cool, Mr Sandhu." Mo grinned at my dad. Then he looked at me and winked.

"Right. That settle then. But you better ringing your dad and tell him you stay here, innit."

"I'll show him where the phone is, Dad," I offered. Man, I wanted to call Dave over as well.

"An' none of you messing 'bout, innit. This a business not a playground, OK?"

"Yes, Dad. Chill out man. We not going to burn it down."

"Any mucking 'bout an' I killing the two pair of you."

"Anything you say, Mr Sandhu. We'll be cool. And thanks for the tenner. I could do with the cash." Mo was sucking up to my dad. Making out he could be trusted. He did it well too, because my old man shut up and left me to show Mo the basics. It was all pretty simple anyway.

****

All through school the following week, I couldn't think of anything except the trials. I was *so* excited.

Dave was acting like he wasn't bothered by it all, but I could tell that he was. He kept on drifting off during lessons and in one lesson he called Mrs Turner, our English teacher, by our male headmaster's name. That had all of us, including Mrs Turner, in stitches. But Dave couldn't even work out what all the fuss was about. He was on another planet, man. Like something out of *Star Wars*.

When it got to Wednesday night and the practice session, all three of us were really up for it. We did about an hour of running and stretching and then played a nine-a-side game, with me and Dave on the same side and Mo on the other.

It was really tiring but Mr Ball, our coach, told us to push a bit harder. "Tomorrow night you lot are going to be up against the best lads in the county and I want you to do well. Bit of effort today will do wonders for your stamina at the trials."

After the practice most of the other lads went home but Mr Ball kept me, Dave and Mo behind, along with a lad called Mike Beech who was coming to the trials too. He was a wicked defender but the main reason I liked him was his sister, Hannah, who was gorgeous.

I'd asked her out loads but she was seeing this other lad and, although I could tell she really liked me, we hadn't been out together. I was always telling Mike to put in a good word in return for me not making him look like a monkey on the footie pitch with my far superior skills. Funnily enough, what I said didn't make him want to help me out.

We were sitting around in the changing rooms at school and Mr Ball was telling us what to expect when we got to the training ground. He went over the different skill tests we'd have to do and what was expected of us.

The trial was going to be a three hour session and there was no guarantee that the four of us would be in the same part of it together. It was more likely that we would be split up and put with lads we didn't know.

I didn't mind that, because the way I saw it, if I was good enough I'd be able to play against anyone.

Mo was nervous but for some reason I felt quite chilled out. I wasn't at the trials yet, though. I knew that, come the next day, I would be wetting myself.

"Right then, lads. That's all I can tell you. The rest is up to you. Just remember that I wouldn't have selected any of you if I didn't think you had what it takes to be a successful footballer."

"Thanks, Mr Ball," I said, feeling good at the way he had praised us.

"That's all right, Jit. I just want all of you to play in the way that I know you can. Who knows, I might end up with a few Premiership stars on my hands!"

"You know it!" replied Dave, grinning. "Man, we are gonna kick some butt."

"Come now, Dave. Save all that for when you actually do get picked."

"Don't count them chickens, man," said Mo, and shook his head.

"Only chicken round here is you, man," replied Dave. "Specially with them legs."

"We'll see, bad boy." Mr Ball cut in, before Dave and Mo went any further. "Right then, lads. I'll see you all after school tomorrow. Get some rest tonight."

With that, Mr Ball let us out and we made our way home, this time making sure we avoided the playing fields. It would be hard to impress at the trials if we'd just been beaten up.

When I got home my old man was in the shop and the smell of freshly fried chips was everywhere. I went in to give him a hand but it was really quiet. After about half an hour, I helped myself to a big portion of chips and some fried chicken and went back into the house, which is behind and above the shop.

My dad closed about half past ten and sat in the living room as my mum made him some tea. She brought it through and then sat down and asked me how school was going.

I told her it was cool and then I asked her if she'd like to have a footballer for a son.

"You know that your dad doesn't want that, beteh. Best you do well at school and not worry about all that."

"But, Mum, what if I end up making millions like Michael Owen? You and Dad wouldn't have to work in the shop any more. Look how tired you are. And Dad."

My mum smiled at me. "You're going to pay for us to retire?"

"Why not? What if I could?"

"You a funny boy sometimes, Baljit," she said. "Anyway, forget about football for just one minute and go to bed. You have school in the morning."

"Yeah, I've got that trip to London."

"Oh yes, your science trip. Do you want me to make you a packed lunch?"

I nearly choked. I'd forgotten about the minor details like packed lunch. It was a good job that my natural talent for getting out of tight spots suddenly woke up. "No, that's OK, Mum. You have enough to do. Can I just have some money so that I can buy lunch?"

She thought about it for a moment. "Yes, that's fine, but don't tell your dad. You know what he's like about wasting money." She looked over at my old man but he had fallen asleep on the sofa. He looked flaked out.

"Don't I just." I smiled. "He's like that character on *Goodness Gracious Me,* man. *I can make it at home!*"

Both of us started laughing at my joke, and that woke my dad up. "Hell you two laughing at? What you planning?"

"Nothing, Dad. Go back to sleep."

I didn't have to tell him. He was already asleep again.

Chapter 5

The Trial

There were about 30 lads at the trial and it started at just after five in the evening.

I was put in a group with some lads from three different schools around the city. One of them was a black lad called Tony Andrews. He played for the same Sunday League side as Dave and Mo and I knew him really well. He was related to Dave and played in the same position as me, central midfield. I think he was as pleased to see me as I was to see him.

The pitch had been divided between four groups and I could see Dave, Mike and Mo but I couldn't speak to them.

The coach, who was called Mr Jones, was giving us instructions about the various skill tests we had to do. They involved dribbling the ball around flag posts, control skills, heading, passing and shooting at targets. We had to start with our weakest foot first, which for me was my left, and then do the whole lot again with the stronger foot.

I was doing OK, apart from when I lost my balance trying to turn and went flying into Tony. I was gutted, but Tony just helped me up, smiling, and told me to forget it and carry on as normal.

After an hour and a half of that, the entire group was split into two teams, and I got to be on the same team as Mo and Tony.

The coaches started an eleven-a-side game on a full-sized pitch with the players that were left out waiting on the sidelines.

Every ten or 15 minutes one of the lads playing was pulled off to allow another one on. I was waiting to go on, and trying to catch my breath after the last skill test. As I watched Dave tear our teams' defence apart, I smiled. It was wicked to see my best mate doing so well.

Mo came off and asked me how it was going and I told him I was fine but a bit nervous. He just shrugged his shoulders and said that he'd had a nightmare. He'd been kicked on the ankle. It had swollen up so much that he couldn't play any more. Our school coach, Mr Ball, took him back into the changing rooms. Mo looked gutted. I felt really bad but I didn't want to let his injury affect my own performance. I had a chance to shine and I was going to take it.

Along both sides of the pitch were various blokes with clipboards making notes about some of the lads. There were about 20 of them, all wearing tracksuits and watching the game really closely. I wondered who they were. Leicester City wouldn't have that many youth team coaches.

When I looked back at the pitch, Dave let fly with a shot from about 20 yards out. It flew into the top corner and he turned and did a little war dance, a big grin all over his face. Then one of the other lads jogged off and I got a tap on my shoulder from one of the Leicester coaches.

"Baljit, your turn, son."

I jogged on and joined my team. Tony was already playing in my position so I slotted in, on his right, and we played together. The other team had some big, strong players and as soon as I touched the ball, one of them took my legs out from behind me. I groaned as I went down and for a moment the wind was knocked out of me.

I lay on the ground, rolling around, thinking my trial was over, but Tony and Dave came and helped me up.

Dave leant towards me, as the referee walked off, and whispered in my ear. "You see that fat redneck who just done you? Recognise him?"

I looked at the player who had fouled me. He did look familiar.

"Last week, man. The lads that chased us. He was the mouthy one."

"Yeah, now I remember. I'm gonna do him when he gets the ball." As I spoke the redneck mouthed the word 'Paki' at me. Then he spat.

"Leave it, Jit. It ain't gonna help you get picked. We'll get him later."

The game restarted and Tony picked up the ball, twisted past a challenge and pushed the ball into space, wanting me to have a shot or play the strikers in.

I read his thoughts and as I gathered the ball, the racist lad tried to tackle me, holding on to my shirt. I put the ball through his legs and broke free, touched it past one of his team mates and saw our striker run into space. I pushed the ball through to him and he placed it just past the keeper to make the score 1–1.

I didn't celebrate. I just shook Tony's hand and went back up the field for the restart.

About five minutes later, I picked the ball up in the midfield and passed it through the air, to the left winger. The ball landed right at his feet and I was well pleased. The winger took on his marker and then had to check back as there was no-one in the box for him to pass to.

I sprinted into the space but he played it behind me, to Tony, who got the ball and curled a shot past their keeper. It was a wicked goal and this time half our team jumped him. We were in the lead. Yes! But as I made my way back to the centre circle the racist lad ran up to me and called me a 'Paki' again.

This time I got really angry and we had a scuffle. The referee was straight over and told us both off. I complained about his racial abuse but the ref just waved me away and the game kicked off. My heart was going ten to the dozen and I was wound up like never before. I wanted to batter the racist loudmouth.

Tony shouted for me to move forward, which I did, as he brought the ball upfield.

Again he skipped past two or three players like they weren't even there and then played the ball to me.

I had my back to the goal, and a defender right up behind me. I faked a turn to my right which the defender followed and instead I went the other way. I was in space, with the goal 25 yards in front of me. I looked for a team mate to pass to. There were two. Something made me ignore them. I wanted to prove that the racist lad hadn't beaten me. I wanted to show him that I was ten times the player that he was. So I just hit the ball.

It flew like an arrow, straight and rising. The ball smashed against the post and flew in. I couldn't believe it. I'd scored. I was on top of the world. My team mates jumped all over me, and then it was back to the centre for the kick off. This time the racist lad tripped me as I went past and called me some more names. Then he spat at me. He missed but the ref saw everything and ran over.

"Right lad, that's it. You're off!"

"But … he …" began the lad, trying to play innocent.

"Racist and abusive language has no place on this pitch, son. You're off. And you can go straight home. You won't be asked back."

The lad went mental and told the ref to 'eff off'. His mates and his school coach had to drag him away. As I stood up I heard the ref tell the coach that he would be reporting the school to the Football Association. The coach went red in the face and stormed off.

Ten minutes later, the final whistle blew and it was all over. My knees were shaking. I was knackered. Dave, Tony, Mike and me walked off together, telling each other we'd done well. Mr Ball told us we were great, even though Tony didn't play for him. It was just a really wicked feeling.

After we had showered and changed,
Mr Ball drove us home, dropping me and Mike
off outside Mo's house, before he took Dave
and Tony back.

Mo was gutted and I found out that the
redneck who'd got at me was the one that had
injured Mo. I tried to tell Mo that we'd had
the last laugh, but he wasn't wearing it. I could
see his point. He hadn't had the chance to
prove himself like I had. I left it at that and
went home, hoping that Mo would feel better
after some sleep. I didn't think he would,
though. I know I wouldn't have.

I got in just after nine, walking through
the chippy to get into the house, rather than
the side door. My dad was sitting behind the
counter reading a copy of the *Sun* newspaper.
Or rather, looking at the pictures. I yawned
at him as a way of saying hello.

"How was your trip, beteh?" he asked me.

"Cool. I'm really tired though."

"Is it raining outside?" Dad was staring at me.

"No, why?" I looked straight back at him.

"Because you having wet hair, Baljit."

Time for me to do a bit of quick thinking. "Yeah, one of the kids thought it would be funny to start a food fight on the back of the coach. I got soaked with bottled water and soft drinks."

I was well pleased with my quick-fire response, but my dad just shook his head. For a moment I was worried, but then he closed his paper, yawned and stood up.

"Telling you what. My day, teacher giving us slipper on back of head for that. World gone soft, Baljit. No wonder all them druggies all over the place."

"Yeah, yeah. I'd love to listen, Dad, but I've heard it all before and I just wanna eat some food and go to bed."

It was my fault. I stood there for far too long. I was distracted when my mum walked out of the back into the shop and just then my dad got a handful of slimy batter and rubbed it into my hair.

"Better getting in bath before you going bed, innit," he said, bursting into laughter along with my mum. I just stood there as batter dripped down my face.

When my mum finally stopped laughing she told me to have a shower while she made me some food. And then she started laughing again till the tears rolled down her cheeks. Insulted by me own parents! I was gutted.

Chapter 6
Hannah

"How do you think the trials went, then?" I asked Dave as we walked out of Burger King in the city centre. It was two days after the session and I had no idea about how we'd done. Mr Ball wouldn't find out until the following week. But that didn't stop me itching to know.

"Dunno, man. I reckon you and me done well. I mean how much more can you do on top of scoring a goal each?" Dave took a big bite of his cheeseburger as he waited for me to reply.

"It ain't just about that though, is it. They were looking for other stuff – like whether we can read the game and that."

"What? Reading? So you mean that whole thing on Thursday wasn't about playing footie?"

"You moron. You know what I meant." I couldn't help laughing, though.

"Just gotta wait till Mr Ball gets the results, man. No use trying to make the future happen today."

"Why not, Mr Know-it-all?" I said, picking out a gherkin from my cheeseburger and throwing it into a nearby bin.

"Er ... well, it wouldn't be the future then, would it."

"Very funny."

We walked down the main shopping street and into a sports shop. I wanted a new pair of trainers and I was hoping to see a wicked pair in their sale. It would be easier to convince my dad to part with the money if he thought it was paying for a bargain. He was tight. I had a good look around but didn't see anything that I liked. Dave got bored watching me pick up every pair of trainers and suggested that we go and play pool, which we did. Anything to get my mind off the trials.

Mo didn't come to school the day after the trials. His ankle was really sore and I think he was feeling down too. I would have been. I wanted to go round to his house to see him but Dave thought it would be better to give him some space so that he could sort himself out.

In the end, I waited until me and Dave had finished playing pool and then I went round to see Mo on my own. His house is only round the corner from mine, and I was hoping he'd want to come round to mine to have a go on my Playstation.

When I got to his house, no-one answered. I rang the bell again and again but it was no use. I gave up and headed home. I had to help my old man get everything ready for the evening.

I spent the rest of the night peeling and chipping potatoes and frying them. It was a very busy night and old Mr Biggs, the nutter, came in as usual.

About half nine, I was behind the counter, wrapping cod and chips when I saw Mike's sister, Hannah, come in. She was with her boyfriend but he looked really angry – like they'd been fighting. She walked up to the counter and smiled at me. "Hi, Jit."

I looked across at her and smiled weakly. I was going red. Man, she was so fit. My old man saw my face and grinned.

"Not going to offer the young lady the reply, Baljit?" he said.

Man, I could have killed him.

"That your real name? Baljit?" asked Hannah.

"Yeah, I don't like it." I watched as her boyfriend just stood there, looking angry. She saw me watching her boyfriend and turned to him.

"You may as well go home, John. I'll ring my brother from here."

"But I can still walk you ..." John looked angry *and* upset.

"No, you can't. I don't want you to." Hannah's voice was really stern, like a teacher telling off a pupil. "I don't wanna see you anymore. I'll ring my brother to come get me and anyway, Jit is one of my best mates. He'll look after me." She winked at me and I smiled back. Man, what a result!

Hannah was splitting up with her boyfriend. And she was in my dad's shop while she was giving him the elbow. There had to be a God.

John stood and looked gutted for another ten minutes before he finally pushed off. Hannah turned to me and asked if she could use my phone. I told her to ask my old man, but she saw my mum coming out the back and asked her. I think she was standing up for women's rights and that. Or trying to be funny. Or both. My mum smiled and asked if she was a friend of mine.

"Yeah, I'm his girlfriend," grinned Hannah.

Well, you could have put a train in my mouth, it fell that wide open. I didn't know what my mum would think about me having a girlfriend, specially one that wasn't Punjabi. Man, what was Hannah playing at?

"Strange, he's never mentioned you before," replied my mum, giving me a funny look.

"She's messing about, Mum," I said, trying to cover my tracks.

"No she ain't," said my dad, butting in and giving me a shock. "She very pretty girl an' all, innit."

I didn't know which way to turn. What was my old man playing at? I was shocked. My mum was quite laid back but I had always thought that my dad was proper traditional.

"Well, you may use the phone ... er ..." began my mum.

"Hannah," I said, helpfully. "I'll show her where it is, Mum."

"Yes, Baljit. You do that. And then I think you and me should have a little talk, beteh." Mum turned away.

Hannah followed me into the house as my old man grinned at me, taking the mick. When we were out of earshot I turned to Hannah. "What was all that about?"

"What?" She pretended to look confused.

"Since when were you my girlfriend?"
I asked.

Hannah just smiled. "So you don't want to
take me out. Funny, that's not what Mike
tells me."

"He ... he told you?" I was horrified.

"Told me? He tells me all the time.
You keep asking him to." She smiled wider.

"What about John?" I asked.

"We've just finished. You just saw it.
I haven't wanted to see him for ages – he just
didn't get the message." She stopped smiling
and looked at me. Expecting something.

"So, are you asking me out or what?" she
said, waiting.

"Er ... yeah. When would you ...?" I was
red like a beetroot. This was better than
scoring a goal at the trials.

"Tomorrow night. We'll go to a film. Call for me at six."

Just like that. Like she had planned it all out before she got to the shop. Nimble as a ninja.

"Er ... cool." I had this strange feeling that I had been targeted, surrounded and captured. Like some kind of army operation. And I had.

"Now, where's your phone?"

I looked at her and felt like I could walk on air. I had to be dreaming. Before I lost any more ground, though, I snapped back into reality.

"Don't worry about calling Mike," I said. "I'll walk you home."

Hannah grinned. "That would be nice."

You're telling me, I thought as I smiled inside and out.

After I had walked Hannah back to her house, I got back in and my mum was waiting for me. She didn't look angry or anything. Just confused. My dad was closing up the shop and I was in the back, with the sacks of potatoes and my mum, who was asking me a load of questions. Who was this girl? Why hadn't I said anything about her before? How long had I been going out with her?

"You know, Baljit, your father and me do not mind if you go out with girls. We are not like some parents. You were born in this country – you are bound to do what your friends do."

"I thought you'd be really angry," I said, not letting on that I had been tricked into going out with Hannah. Not that I minded. Not at all.

"Angry? Why would we be angry? She seems like a nice girl. Do her parents mind that you are not white?"

"Nah, I doubt it. I've met them before. They're really cool. She's Mike's sister, Mum."

"Mike? Oh, Mike, that nice boy that comes in now and then."

"Yeah."

As I answered my dad walked in. As soon as he saw me he grinned again.

"Look like you owing your old dad one, innit. Fix you up with nice girl."

"I thought you wanted me to find a nice Asian girl," I said.

He laughed. "I wanting you to make something of yourself. Up to you about girls an' that, Baljit."

"Man, you are full of surprises, you two." I nodded at him and my mum.

"Bit like that girl, innit."

"Yeah, she sure took me by surprise, Dad."

"Better thanking me then, Baljit." He looked at my mum who looked even more confused.

"What are you two talking about?" she asked.

"Never mind, Mum. I'm sure Dad will tell you. Cheers, Dad."

I shot off into the house and rang Dave to tell him what had happened. I was well excited. I was going on a date with Mike's sister. Me. Every boy at our school fancied her. I was the man.

Chapter 7
Result!

I was at school the following Tuesday, talking to Dave and Mo, telling them for about the tenth time what happened on my date with Hannah.

Dave was trying to make me admit that we had done more than just kiss, but he was wrong. We did snog loads but nothing else, and even if there was anything else to tell, I wasn't about to tell Dave. He was like a newspaper, one of those cheap ones that spreads nasty gossip everywhere. He was like a girl, in fact. Always chatting. He pestered me all lunchtime until I called him a 'grass'.

"Man, I ain't no grass. Don't be callin' me no rat. Never said anything to anyone," Dave protested, and then he shut up.

If I hadn't known him as well as I did, I might have thought that I'd upset him, but he was just playing with me. Trying to pull my leg. I ignored him and asked Mo if his ankle was better.

"Yeah, the swelling's gone but I'm still angry. That lad was out to break my leg."

"I know. The ref sussed him though. In the end." I was trying to make Mo feel better but it wasn't working.

"Well, I'm still gonna do him if I see him." Mo's face was set hard with anger.

"He ain't worth it, Mo," I warned him. "Let it go. There's bound to be another trial soon."

"Easy for you to say, man. You and Dave got to show what you could do."

I was going to carry on but I didn't want to end up arguing with Mo about the trials. It wasn't worth falling out with my best mate over football. And the mood Mo was in, I knew he'd lose his temper.

In the end, I just changed the subject and asked him if he'd seen Mike anywhere. Mo told me he was by the tennis courts. I told Mo that I'd see him in English and walked over to where Mike was standing with two of his mates. "Thanks, Mike, for talking to Hannah."

Mike just grinned at me. "That's all right. Man, she ain't stopped talking about you," he told me.

"What, really?" I was chuffed.

"Yeah – must be love." He laughed.

"Don't take the mick, Mike boy," I replied, smiling.

"Mr Ball told me that he knows about the trials," said Mike. Suddenly the whole focus of my attention shifted.

"What? When?" I was all excited again.

"This morning. He's gonna get us together just after lunch."

"Oh man, I'd better go and tell Dave." I told Mike I'd see him later and went back to where Dave was standing.

He saw the look on my face and raised an eyebrow. "Don't tell me you've been snogging Hannah again?" he said.

"Nah. Just shut up and listen Dave."

"Yes, boss." He laughed.

"Mr Ball knows about the trials, man."
I knew that would get him to stop clowning
around.

"What?" Dave's eyes had lit up.

"Yeah, Mike just told me. Ball's going to
get us together after lunch."

"Wicked. And we'll get out of English for a
bit."

Mr Ball called us to an empty classroom 20
minutes later. My heart was in my mouth.
Mo was the only one out of the four of us who
went to the trials that wasn't there. Dave was
already talking about who he was going to
play for and where he was going to buy a flat,
what car he was going to drive. Honest,
sometimes even I thought he was crazy.

Mike was just standing in the same spot,
his ears, neck and throat a bright shade of
scarlet.

Ball was holding a letter for each of us and another that he had opened. "Well, lads. Let's see what we've got." Mr Ball looked at Mike first.

"Mike, you've been asked to attend a second trial at Leicester City next week. This one is being run by City's youth team manager, so you've done well, son. Congratulations."

Mike smiled from ear to ear. He was over the moon.

"Straight back to your classroom, Mike. I'll speak to you again tomorrow night."

After Mike had left, Mr Ball turned to Dave, smiling. He told Dave that the blokes who we'd seen at the side of the pitch at the trials were coaches from various teams.

They had been there looking for new talent for their youth academies. There had even been one from Ajax, who are based in Amsterdam! Talk about cool.

"Dave, you're going to be getting invitations from Leicester City, Coventry, Aston Villa, and I know this will make your head grow bigger than ever, Arsenal."

Dave just stood there. For once he had nothing to say. At all. I think he was in shock. I was. Arsenal were one of the best teams in Europe and Dave was being offered a place at their academy.

Mr Ball handed him a letter. "That is an official invitation from Arsenal Football Club. Your parents have to give their consent. Well done, son. I hope you can get them to sign you up."

Dave still hadn't said anything. Ball told him that he'd have to go to London for a month in the summer to attend a pre-academy school. Dave just blinked. At me. At Mr Ball.

And then he smiled, slowly. Ball told him to go back to his lesson. Dave nodded and walked towards the door. As he went out into the corridor, he gave a loud cry, like an Apache warrior.

Mr Ball laughed and turned to me. Man, I thought my heart was going to come flying out of the top of my head. But then what if I hadn't been picked by anyone? What if ...

"Jit, well, what can I say to you, son?" began Mr Ball, looking all stern. I thought I was going to get a telling off. But then he smiled.

"You, young man, along with your friend Tony, must have gold in those feet of yours." He laughed.

"What you on about, Mr Ball? Did we do OK?" I was getting nervous. I thought I was going to be sick.

"Tony and yourself have been invited to second trials by every coach that attended, son."

I nearly *did* throw up and I had to swallow hard.

"But, two teams in particular want to see you both right away. Arsenal and Liverpool."

The last team name sent my whole world into a spin. L-I-V-E-R-P-O-O-L. My team. My boys. I had to swallow again.

"Now, I spoke to the youth team manager at Liverpool over the weekend. This envelope has your invitation letter in it. But they want to sign both you and Tony up, subject to some medical tests."

"What ..." I couldn't speak, so I just shut up.

"So I've been in touch with your parents and passed on the number of Liverpool's ..."

"Oh, hell!"

"What's the matter, Jit? I know it's a lot to take in."

"It's not that, Mr Ball. You don't understand. They don't know that I went to a trial – my parents – they don't know."

I was in trouble. I had lied to them and now they'd found out. There was no way they would give their consent to anything now. I told Mr Ball what had happened and all he did was smile. *Smile*! There I was about to get grounded for life for lying and all Mr Ball could do was smile.

I went back to my English lesson trying to think of a way out of my problem but all I could think of was how much grief I was in.

After school, I don't think my feet touched the ground on my way home. I was going to take my time getting back but I decided it was better to tell the truth and face the music.

After all, even though I'd lied, it had worked out well in the end. I was being asked to sign up for Liverpool. Surely my parents wouldn't hold the lie against me after that?

When I got in, however, I lost all confidence. My mum was in the shop and gave me a stern look when I walked in. "Baljit. Your father is upstairs waiting for you. I think you have something to tell us, beteh."

"Look, Mum, I only did it because ..."

"Go and talk to your father. I'm just going to get some more chips cut and then I'll come up."

As I walked up the stairs, I thought to myself, *that's it, I'm done for.* I went to my room and dropped my bag and the letter on the bed. I walked slowly back down to the living room, praying that my dad was in a good mood.

As I walked through the door, I saw my dad standing, holding a letter similar to the one Mr Ball had given to me. I was about to start talking when my dad held up his hand. "Don't even start, Baljit. I have had a very strange letter today, from someone at Liverpool."

"Look, Dad, I can explain." I was finished.

"So science trip mean playing the football, then?"

My mum walked in just as I tried to get another word in.

"You didn't tell us about this," said my dad, waving the letter. My mum walked over to where he was and stood next to him.

"We are ... well, Baljit, we are both ..."

They both looked at me and then suddenly my mum smiled and my dad looked like he had tears in his eyes.

"We are both very proud of you, beteh."

I nearly fell over in shock!

"You did lie to us," said my mum. "That is wrong, Baljit. You should have just told us."

"We never knowing it was this serious – Liverpool's coach tell me you are very good. Bright future."

"But I ... I thought you didn't want ..."

"I never want you to waste your life. This," he waved the letter again, "this not wasting life, Baljit. This something to be very proud of. To tell you the truth, your teacher, Mr Ball phone me on Saturday. I known since then."

"But why didn't you *say* something?"

"Couldn't surprise you then, could we?" So that was why Mr Ball had smiled when I told him about the lie.

And then he came over and gave me a hug, followed by my mum. They were both in tears and so was I.

"So, I can go?"

"Too right you going, beteh. You can pay for us retiring, innit." My dad grinned and picked up a tennis ball that was on the sofa. He threw it at me.

Then he grinned even wider. "Head it back, beteh. On me turban, innit!"

Barrington Stoke would like to thank all its readers for commenting on the manuscript before publication and in particular:

Nosheen Asif
Della Bartram
Mandeep Bassi
Anthea Beale
Kalsuma Begum
Rothna Begum
Wahida Begum
Lee Bond
Joanne Bruce
Kerrie Bullough
Melissa Collins
Mandy Collister
Nicky Crowther
Hasika Desai
Ekta Dhameja
Sukhjit Dhillon
Dhamiyat Singh Fail
Rahul Ghadiali
Rikesh Ghadiali
Fatima Ghumra
Jasdeep Kaur Gill
Sandeep Gill
Lauren Graham
Barry Greenlaw

Gurpreet Harrad
Tabusum Hussain
Lyndsey Johnson
Lucy Jones
Harprit Kaur
Arefa Khayam
Alastair Kleissner
Moira Kleissner
Simon Lane
Gurjit Kaur Mandair
Rebecca Mattingly
Andrew May
Linda McDougall
Frina Mistry
Heena Mistry
Vanisha Mistry
Amisha Morar
Carolyn Mortimore
Phil Neal
Clara O'Brien
Laura O'Leary
Dipesh Patel
Jayshree Patel
Kajal Patel

Kapil Patel
Sabera Patel
Stephanie Pears
Renu Kaur Purewal
Hassan Rahman
Satvir Kaur Rai
Dhiren Shah
Hamid Shahid
Hannah Sharpe
Baljeet Singh Shetra
Gurjeet Shetra
Sandeep Singh Sian
Evelyn Smith
Sonal Solanki
Annette Speak
Aqila Syed
Sheereen Talati
Monica Thakrar
Becky Thumpston
Mark Wilson
Vanessa Wood
Fahima Yasmin
Robert Young

Become a Consultant!

Would you like to give us feedback on our titles before they are published? Contact us at the e-mail address below – we'd love to hear from you!

E-mail: info@barringtonstoke.co.uk
Website: www.barringtonstoke.co.uk

Great reads – no problem!

Barrington Stoke books are:

Great stories – from thrillers to comedy to spine-chilling horror, and all by the best writers around!

No hassle – fast reads with no boring bits, and a brilliant story that doesn't let go of you till the last page.

Short – the perfect size for a fast, fun, satisfying read.

We use our own font and paper to make it easier for dyslexic people to read our books too. And we ask teenagers like you, who want a no-hassle read, to check every book before it's published.

That way, we know for sure that every Barrington Stoke book is a great read for everyone.

Check out www.barringtonstoke.co.uk for more info about Barrington Stoke and our books!

BALI'S BOOKS!

Revenge of the Number Two

"It was very funny and the use of slang is good!
I give this book 10 out of 10."
Jamie, age 14

What's Your Problem?

"I thought that the book was great. It reminds people
that racism is still going on."
Amazon review

Two-Timer

"I brought the book straight home and read it
from start to finish. I really enjoyed it.
I had never read a book in years."
Josh, via email

Dream On

"The book was very exciting, never got boring
and was very moving."
Amazon review

Also by the same author ...

What's Your Problem?

Jaspal is a city boy and life in a village just isn't for him. And he's the only Asian teenager around. When the insults begin, Jaspal's dad tells him that things will be OK – but the racism just gets worse.

Soon it becomes clear that things will never get better. Jaspal's life will never be the same again ...

You can order **What's Your Problem?** directly from our website at **www.barringtonstoke.co.uk**

Also by the same author ...

Two-Timer

Harj has no girlfriend and no hope, as his friends like to keep telling him. So when not one but *two* of the fittest girls in school ask him out, how can he say no? At first he feels bad about cheating on them ... then he starts to enjoy it. Soon lying is as easy as insulting his sister!

But will his luck run out?

How long can he play the game?

You can order **Two-Timer** directly from our website at **www.barringtonstoke.co.uk**

Also by the same author ...

Revenge of the Number Two

Life at school's never easy but for Kully there's no hope. His school life has gone down the toilet – all because of the time he didn't go. To the toilet.

Will Kully always be "Mr Number Two"? Or can he get his revenge on the bullies who make his life so bad? It'll take two cute girls ... a rudeboy teacher ... a goat (don't ask about the goat) ... and an awful lot of poo.

A wicked, gross-out comedy!

You can order *Revenge of the Number Two* directly from our website at **www.barringtonstoke.co.uk**